Also by Jan Springer

Pleasure Bound
A Hero's Welcome
A Hero Escapes
A Hero Betrayed
A Hero's Kiss
A Hero Wanted
Captive Heroes

Pleasure Bound Boxed Set
Pleasure Bound : COMPLETE SERIES SciFi Erotic Romance Boxed
Set

Tentacles Shifter Erotic Romance
Taken by Him

The Key Club
A Merry Menage Christmas
Sophie's Menage
Jewel's Menage
Jaxie's Menage

The Outlaw Lovers
Jude Outlaw
The Claiming

Colter's Revenge
Tyler's Woman
Resistance
The Outlaw Lovers
Alpha Outlaws Boxed Set

Vampira
Sweet Heat
Dark Heat
Wet Heat
Crimson Heat

Standalone
A Touch of Menage Boxed Set
Shades of Menage Boxed Set
Naughty Girl Desires Boxed Set
Nice Girl Naughty
Sinderella Sexy
The Biker and The Bride
The Fire Within
Bared to Him
Pleasure Bound : A Futuristic Adult Romance Boxed Set
Merry Menage Kisses Boxed Set
Inner Girl Rising
Stripped Naked
Risqué Girl Delights Boxed Set
A Holiday Menage
Ménage À Trois
A Hitman for Hannah
Billionaire Boyfriend

Edible Delights
Vampira
Toygasm

Watch for more at www.janspringer.com.

Christmas Lovers

Jan Springer

Sergeant Connor Jordan, wounded overseas and sent back to the States to recuperate, just cannot stop fantasizing about the sexy nurse who cared for him. When his brothers give him a holiday gift certificate to Kidnap Fantasies, a top-secret fantasy organization, Connor knows he'll use their gift, if only to help him forget his wickedly delicious attraction to Nurse Sparks.

Nurse Tania Sparks has always been purely professional with her injured soldiers...until sinfully sexy Connor Jordan enters her hospital. He makes her body throb with an intense desire she's never known before. The last thing she wants is to get involved with the injured warrior. So what's a woman supposed to do to relieve her naughty frustrations? Call Kidnap Fantasies and have them supply her with a look-alike man who'll help her forget her sexy soldier...

When Tania and Connor unexpectedly come together at a secluded mountain chalet, their love explodes in a ménage of passion, sensuous desires and a happily forever after.

Contains ménage scenes.

Christmas Lovers

Jan Springer
Published by Spunky Girl Publishing
Copyright 2015 Jan Springer
2nd edition
Edited by Julie Naughton

License Notes

This ebook is licensed for your personal use only.
The ebook may not be re-sold or given away to other people.
If you would like to share your ebook with another person, please purchase an additional copy for each recipient.
Thank you for respecting the hard work of this author.
This is a work of fiction. Characters, places, settings, and events presented in this book are purely of the author's imagination and bear no resemblance to any actual person, living or dead or to any actual events, places, and/or settings.

Newsletter

Hi! If you would like to get an email when my books are released, you can sign up here:

Newsletter: http://ymlp.com/xguembmugmgb

Your emails will never be shared and you can unsubscribe whenever you like.

Dedication

Dedicated to wounded soldiers and the wonderful nurses who care for them.

May God bless and protect you.

Prologue

Several months earlier...

Pain.

So much pain he could just scream as he lay helpless in the U.S. military hospital bed they'd brought him to.

He remembered the nurse, the one with the soft voice who he'd immediately fallen in love with. She'd said something about burns and broken bones to his lower legs. A shrapnel wound near his heart. A concussion. Temporary blindness.

Shit, he was a freaking mess, wasn't he?

But he'd been stabilized overseas. Brought back to the States at the direction of his brothers. They'd pulled heavy-duty strings getting him here so fast. They'd wanted him recuperating close to home, not in some foreign country.

Snatches of memories sifted through his mind. Memories of an explosion. Searing heat. Too-bright orange flames.

He remembered the agonized cries. His buddies' cries, the feeling of helplessness. The terror and then, thankfully, the darkness.

Sergeant Connor Jordan jerked involuntarily as a feminine hand smoothed over his hot forehead.

Nurse Sparks, his Florence Nightingale.

She was back on duty, and he felt relieved. She always smelled so damned good and her soft touches were quick to settle his uneasiness. Quick to make the memories of that horrible day disappear.

"I can see they took the bandages off your eyes."

Her voice sounded so sexy. Intimate. As if he were the only man in the world for her. She moved into his field of vision and he finally saw her for the first time.

Sexy chocolate-brown eyes and a wild tangle of dark-brown hair greeted him. Her plump cheeks were flushed a pretty pink as if she'd just come in from a brisk walk.

Her mouth...perfection.

The sweet knot that had settled into his lower belly the first time he'd heard her voice a few days ago turned into something else. Turned into a scorching, driving need. A craving to have her soft, warm lips wrap around his erection.

"You can see me okay, soldier?"

Soldier, her nickname for him. He'd bet she called all the boys that.

He nodded.

She smiled. Dimples exploded in her cheeks and he fell in love with her all over again.

Oh man! Was he already experiencing the infamous Florence Nightingale Syndrome soldiers talked about? Had he fallen in love with the nurse who was caring for him?

Fuck, if that were the case, then he was in really big trouble.

And so was his cock.

Chapter One

Several months later...

"Time for your sponge bath, soldier." Her soft voice drifted out of the darkness and Sergeant Connor Jordan's eyes flickered open to find Nurse Sparks standing there, the green privacy curtain drawn around his hospital bed.

At the hungry look sparkling in her brown eyes, his shaft hardened into a hot and pulsing rod of lust. He gritted his teeth as his balls tightened with arousal.

He knew she wanted him. He wanted her too. Had seen the need, the desperation to be fucked every time she came in at night to give him a sponge bath. He wanted to make love to her so bad he would do it the minute she gave him permission.

Swallowing back his excitement, he watched her slide the basin filled with steaming water onto the nearby table, then pulled away the blanket covering him. Gently, she lifted the hospital gown and her eyes widened slightly as she saw his full-blown erection.

Licking her lips with that cute pink tongue of hers, she sat down on the edge of his bed.

"I can see you're feeling much better, soldier."

"I always feel damned good when you come for a visit, Florence."

She smiled at the nickname he'd given her after the famous nurse who'd taken care of wounded soldiers during the 1800s.

"Perhaps I should take care of your newest...medical condition?" she said softly. He held his breath as warm feminine fingers wrapped tightly around the base of his standing-at-attention erection. Her other hand began a rough massage of his scrotum, her fingers manipulating the swollen balls inside.

Fuck! She was good!

She touched her lips to the tip of his purple plum-shaped cock head then gave him a couple of slow, seductive licks.

"How's that feel, soldier boy?" She turned her head and smiled over at him. Lust glittered in those baby browns.

"Feels damn fine, Florence," he managed to croak.

"Want more?"

He nodded eagerly and watched as his favorite nurse parted her full red lips and the tip of his shaft disappeared into her hot, moist mouth.

Oh man! He loved the feel of her mouth wrapped around his sensitive rod. Loved the way she hollowed out her cheeks and began a wicked sucking motion that rocked him right to his core.

Slurping sounds ripped through the air as her head bobbed up and down his shaft, the sensual movements sending her brown tangled curls into an untamed flurry.

She devoured him like a true professional. Slid his penis out of her lusciously tight mouth and then back in again. He groaned as she used her sharp teeth on him, nipping his foreskin every once in a while. The friction made his swollen flesh jump, made his breaths come harsher, faster. He cried out as her long fingers increased the pressure against his swollen sac.

The pleasure spread. His body grew hot, tight. Blood pumped into his and balls. He knew he was on the verge of coming. Knew this was going to be a fantastic orgasm.

So fucking big!

"Hey! Earth to Connor. Earth to Connor."

At the sound of his oldest brother Ethan's voice, Connor's fantasy vanished, leaving him with painfully hard balls and one hell of an erection. A chorus of rowdy laughter, intermingling with jolly Christmas music, crashed in around him. He blinked and shook his head, remembering he'd been released from the hospital over a month ago and his three brothers had brought him to this noisy bar to celebrate the anniversary.

"Where the hell did you zone out to? Florence Nightingale land again?" Ethan laughed as his brothers all leaned forward to watch him curiously from their barstools.

Florence Nightingale, Connor's nickname for Nurse Sparks, the gorgeous nurse who'd cared for him at the military hospital in Maryland. His brothers had all kidded him about her. Had joked with her every time she'd come to give him a sponge bath or change the dressings on his burns and wounds or administer his meds.

"By the smile on his face he had to be thinking about her. Hell, if it had been me in that hospital bed and totally at her mercy, I'd have gotten that cute, sexy nurse to—" Ethan shut Jake up with a sharp elbow to Jake's side.

"Don't worry, bro, we have the cure for what ails you," his youngest brother Lee said. The sound of his hand slapping against the bar in front of him caught his attention.

A fancy midnight-blue brochure with sharp pink words "Kidnap Fantasies Inc." sat there.

"What is it?"

"Our Christmas gift to you, man," Ethan said softly.

He noticed his brothers were now silent, their faces serious.

"We thought you would die from your injuries, man," Lee said. His green eyes were intense, his voice thick with emotion.

"Yeah, man. We thought we'd lost you over there." Jake frowned and shoved a hand through his long brown hair.

Christ! Did he detect tears in all their eyes?

"C'mon. I wasn't that bad."

"Ever the fucking modest one, aren't you?" Jake shook his head. "They said you were dead twice on the operating table."

"Do I look dead?" Connor chuckled.

Fuck! He sure didn't feel dead, especially with this swollen shaft he'd been toting around since laying his ears and eyes on Nurse Tania Sparks.

"Enough of this mushy shit," Lee continued. "We pooled together and got you a Christmas holiday sexfest compliments of Kidnap Fantasies—it's a top-secret fantasy business."

Connor couldn't help but chuckle. "So much for it being top secret if all you guys know about it."

"We've all taken a vow of secrecy. We trust you won't blow the organization's cover." Lee grinned.

"He wouldn't dream of it." Jake chuckled. "Especially when they make every man's wildest fantasy come true."

Every man's wildest fantasy come true? Hmm, he could think of quite a lot of fantasies he wouldn't mind trying out on a certain brown-haired nurse.

More hot blood pumped into his already tight and painful shaft. He made a move to pick up the brochure but his brothers shook their heads as the bartender slapped another round of frothing beers onto the countertop.

"No way, buddy brother. Look at that brochure and answer the questionnaire on your own time—right now, we party about you getting out of that hospital. Right, boys?"

"Party! Party! Party!" the others all chimed in.

Connor reluctantly let the brochure drop back onto the bar. Partying was suddenly the last thing he felt like doing. He'd rather go back to his apartment and check out what kind of a place would dare to advertise they could make his fantasies come true.

* * * * *

After drinking with his brothers into the wee hours of the morning Connor excused himself and went back to his apartment, took a cold shower, toweled off and climbed naked into bed.

He winced at the sight of his scarred legs, compliments of the burns. He still felt occasional bursts of pain when he walked, but he'd healed quite nicely with the help of the physiotherapists, massage therapists and the doctors and nurses.

Especially one particular nurse. A sexy nurse he'd fantasized about for too damn long.

Spying the Kidnap Fantasies brochure he'd set down on the nearby table he grabbed it and flipped it open.

His pulse began to race.

Ménages. BDSM. Sex-Slave Training. Kidnap scenarios. Whatever your wish, we will fill your desires. Complete the enclosed questionnaire and let our discreet Kidnap Fantasies Inc. set you free.

Yeah, he'd be set for life if he could get ahold of his beauty and live out his fantasies with her. Since that would never happen...he'd have to be content with this brochure and see what they could offer.

Flipping through the pages, he felt his cock hardening and his balls swelling as he gazed at the explicit pictures. There were intimate photos of women fucking women and men fucking men, group sex and plain vanilla sex with a couple.

It would be a waste if he didn't follow through on his brothers' gift certificate to this company. Maybe if he ordered a woman who looked like Nurse Sparks he might be able to fuck her out of his system? He could even request having sex with a man. His cock twitched wildly at that idea. Hell, it wasn't as if he hadn't fantasized about it. No one would have to know.

Maybe he could even ask for a ménage à trois?

He inhaled an aroused breath as his fantasies quickly began to take hold.

Shit! Where was that questionnaire? He flipped to the middle of the brochure and ripped it out.

Grabbing a pen from the nearby bedside table, he began to answer the questions.

Name—Connor Jordan

Age—25

Sex—Male

Sexual preferences—m/m, f/m/m

Sexual experiences—A handful of women.

He scanned down the questions and hesitated at the section of physical preferences for his partner or partners. Putting pen to paper he eagerly wrote out Nurse Tania's description and left the man's description open.

By the time he was finished with all the intimate questions of what he wanted to happen during his Christmas sexfest his shaft was so hard he swore he would explode.

Every nerve ending in his body was on fire as he envisioned Nurse Tania standing naked in front of him. She'd have generous breasts with big pink nipples that would taste like lollipops when he suckled her.

Throwing the brochure and questionnaire aside, his hand went down to squeeze and gently twist his scrotum. He could feel his swollen balls in his sac. Could feel his cock pulse beneath his fingers as he pumped his stiff, purplish flesh nice and slow.

Oh yeah, Nurse Sparks would welcome him into her arms. Her hot, naked breasts would squish nicely against his chest and he'd slide his rock-hard cock deep into her tight, wet pussy in one solid thrust. He'd moan as her slick, wet heat enveloped his thick, long shaft.

He'd make her cry for mercy as he made her climax over and over again.

Having the fantasy of Nurse Sparks firmly in hand, so to speak, Connor came so hard on a guttural groan that stars burst behind his closed eyelids.

Oh yeah, he was definitely going to give Kidnap Fantasies a try.

Chapter Two

Three days later...

The mournful sound of yet another soldier moaning in pain chased Nurse Tania Sparks into the empty elevator of the U.S. Army hospital. She hated leaving her wounded boys. They needed her, especially now as the Christmas holidays were here.

She also knew if she didn't take some time off, she would start making some serious life-threatening mistakes. She'd almost made one last week when she'd pulled a double shift and almost given a patient the wrong medication. Thank God, she'd caught it. But next time she might not be so lucky.

The warning signs were there. If she didn't take a break from all this stress, she'd be well on her way to burnout city.

Been there. Done that. Not going back, thank you very much!

And the last thing she wanted to do was spend time with her family this Christmas. She was moody and bitchy thinking about how stupid she'd been by letting her sexy soldier get away.

Originally, she'd thought to work through the Christmas holidays, dropping in at Mom and Pop's for Christmas dinner. The rest of the time, she'd planned on putting all her energies into helping her soldiers forget they'd be spending Christmas in the hospital instead of at home. She'd hoped work would help her forget Sergeant Jordan. It hadn't.

Sergeant Jordan.

The man whose bright-green eyes made her catch her breath every time she'd looked at him. The one whose full lips she'd craved to kiss. The one whose mouth-watering, ultra-huge, heavy cock she'd lifted while she'd given him sponge baths when he'd first come to the hospital.

Even his name had sounded sexy.

Sergeant Connor Jordan. The man she'd let get away.

She didn't know how she knew it, but instincts kept insisting he might have been the one for her. They'd gotten along so well during his recovery. They didn't even have to talk, and they'd know each other's moods. She'd even been able to read the hunger in his gaze as he'd watched her every move like some predatory animal wanting to mate with her.

She couldn't deny there was a sexual energy zapping the air between them, but she was a professional and had never acted upon it...except for those delicious sponge baths. The sponge baths had been rather intimate. Okay so they'd both enjoyed them a little too much.

She'd taken too much pleasure in wrapping her fingers around his thick shaft and feeling the heavy weight of his member in her hands while she'd bathed his scrotum and other intimate parts.

Even when Connor's rowdy brothers had come to visit, she hadn't missed their elbow nudges or the huge smiles they threw her way when she walked into Connor's hospital room.

Shit! Now that she thought about it, even her fellow nurses had commented on what a cute couple they would make. She'd never felt so sexually attracted to a man before. Maybe she should have said something to Connor. Should have followed through on the sexual attraction.

Sadness enveloped her as she remembered how professional she'd acted with him. In the end, she'd let him go with nothing but a tight hug and a peck on the cheek. When he'd left, she'd cried her eyes out in the nurses' lounge for hours.

It had been just over a month since he'd been gone. He'd never come back or even called. Not that she'd expected him to.

The sound of the elevator doors opening ripped her from her sadness. Stepping out into the deserted hospital parking garage her neck tingled a warning a split second before two shadowy figures dressed in black parkas suddenly stepped in front of her. Icy tendrils slithered up her spine as she moved to get around them. They barred her way. Both wore smug grins.

Shit! Was this a robbery? Attempted rape? Or could it be...them.

The familiar charge of adrenaline screamed through her.

"Nurse Tania Sparks, we presume," one of the men said sharply.

It *was* them. She relaxed, if only a bit. She didn't recognize their faces. She never did. They always sent the new ones. Someone she wouldn't suspect as being part of the organization.

But whoever came for her, she never went down without a fight. When the men reached for her, she managed to elbow the closest one in the stomach. A direct hit, if his gasp of pain was an indication.

"You little bitch!" The other one reached for her. She tried to elbow him too, but he anticipated her move and wrenched her arms painfully behind her back, effectively disabling her.

The one she'd socked in the stomach came around in front of her.

Pain and anger glistened in his eyes. Oh yeah, she'd gotten him good. Served him right for not being careful.

"You really shouldn't go around hitting men you don't know," he hissed.

"You shouldn't go around picking on women you don't know," she retorted, and braced herself as his hand came up and he gently brushed the back of his knuckles along her jaw.

"Very nice. Very nice. I bet you'll be a really good fuck."

She twisted against the guy holding her arms. Tried to get free. He was way too strong.

Shit! She was getting too old for this.

She tensed as the screech of tires came from around a nearby corner. A split-second later a white van pulled up.

Every cell in her body screamed at her to pull herself free before they dragged her into the vehicle. But she was so paralyzed from the fantastic rush of adrenaline screaming through her she could barely fight them as they pushed her into the van and forced her to sit on a bench seat.

Her breath came hard and fast as her kidnappers stared at her. Their eyes sparkled with lust, making their intensions quite clear.

"Please, stay awhile, Nurse Sparks, but first...take off all your clothes."

* * * * *

One day later...

Lusciously hot water cocooned Tania's muscles. She sat naked in the steaming outdoor hot tub on the balcony of the tiny two-story log chalet and watched her breath turn a frosty white as it collided with the cold Canadian Rocky Mountain winter air. Snowflakes swirled madly around her in the quickly descending darkness. The flakes that weren't devoured by the heat of the tub dove past the chalet and plummeted into the nearby valley, adding themselves to snow-covered pine trees or crashing against the exposed jagged rocks of the nearby mountainside.

The sight would literally be breathtaking, but right then, all she could do was wince at the sore muscles that protested movement in various parts of her body and relish the sweet fullness of the butt plug sitting snugly in her ass.

She'd been thrilled when Kidnap Fantasies had contacted her so quickly after she'd requested an assignment for this Christmas weekend.

Having herself kidnapped had always been a thrill-seeking adventure for her. When she needed a break from her high-stress job, she would put in a request with the top-secret company she sometimes worked for. They delivered dependable males to kidnap her and take her to her assignment of servicing a man or a woman, whatever she was in the mood for at the time.

Her kidnappings were always realistic and unexpected. The rush of being abducted left her terribly horny afterward and it allowed her to ease quicker into her assignments.

For this gig, the men who'd kidnapped her had told her to remove her clothing. She'd been instructed to lie on the bench seat with her legs in portable stirrups where they'd been able to give her an intimate vaginal and anal inspection on the go, along with blood tests.

Kidnap Fantasies had a mobile lab and got their lab results quickly. They never took any chances with their employees or clients' sexual health, and she was subjected to frequent medical examinations to make sure she was clean of sexually transmitted diseases.

After the intimate exam, she'd been put on a flight to Calgary, met by a Kidnap Fantasies employee and brought to this cute little place on the mountainside.

Here, she'd spend the entire Christmas-long holiday weekend, enjoying a no-strings sexual relationship with a stranger. She knew she'd be safe with her clients, because they were also screened for any medical or psychological problems just as she was.

Up until this time, she'd enjoyed her secret kidnap fetish and odd sex life.

But now as she sat soaking in the hot tub awaiting the stranger, all she could think about was her green-eyed sexy soldier.

* * * * *

Later that same night...

Connor waved goodbye to the Kidnap Fantasies escort named Santana who'd picked him up at the Calgary airport and driven him to this log chalet nestled in the Canadian Rockies.

Because of the darkness, he couldn't see the scenic mountains, but his guide reassured him they were all around them and tomorrow he'd get an awesome view from the chalet's numerous arched windows.

So there he stood. A couple thousand feet up on the side of a mountain with suitcase in his chilly hand as he watched the red taillights of the KF car disappear down the recently plowed mountainside road.

Despite his nervousness and the sharp snowflakes biting his face, he grinned at the swirls of smoke rushing out of the two chimneys of the small two-story building. Illuminated by a handful of outdoor lights, it was obvious the woman who would be his to do with as he pleased during the Christmas holiday weekend was already here.

He wondered what kind of woman would give up her holidays to spend time with a complete stranger. Hell, she was probably someone just as hard up for some hot-and-heavy sex and a couple of cozy evenings by the fire as he was.

The chalet had been built with square-hewn logs that had turned silver-gray with time. Pale-blue shutters and miniature white Christmas lights adorned each arched window. A cranberry-colored door decorated with garland beckoned him a welcome.

Connor took a deep breath to steady his nerves.

Kidnap Fantasies had set everything up within forty-eight hours of his calling the number on the brochure requesting pickup of the questionnaire. He'd given them a delicious outline of what he'd like to try and the type of woman he wanted.

The fantasy, he had no doubt they could fulfill. But he knew the woman would never be like Nurse Sparks. No one could be like his cute nurse.

Maybe having some hot-and-heavy sex with a Nurse Sparks look-alike would get the real nurse out of his system.

Yeah right. And he was Santa Claus.

At the front door he noticed the erotic-shaped knocker made out of brass. It was shaped like a woman's breast. It made him smile and a little of his nervousness slipped away at the amusing sight. Grabbing the gold ring hanging off the plump metal nipple, he lifted the heavy handle and knocked a couple of times.

He waited.

No answer.

He knocked again. Still no answer.

Great. So much for a warm welcoming committee.

He tried the door handle that looked like a man's penis and the door opened.

Well, here goes.

A blast of warm gingerbread-scented air greeted him as he lugged his small suitcase into the tiny foyer and shut the door behind him. When he turned around, his breath caught at the rustic sight.

The open design was simple. Log walls were stained a warm brown and chinked in with cement. An overstuffed bright-red leather sofa sat beneath a large arched window, which gave him a great glimpse of the miniature snowdrifts settling against the night-darkened windowpanes.

Guilt shifted through him the instant he spied a six-foot Christmas tree standing near a wide set of wooden stairs that led to a loft.

Maybe he should have stayed back in Maryland and had Christmas with his brothers and parents? Nah, he didn't want to coddled and cooed over by his family. They'd been so overprotective of him since he'd come back from Iraq that he'd begun to feel smothered.

His brothers would make his excuses for him. They knew where he'd gone. Knew what he'd needed.

From where he stood, he glimpsed a loft above. Guarded by a white railing, it had a white-planked ceiling with cranberry-colored log beams. He bet that's where the bed would be. Maybe the woman would be there, waiting for him.

He stifled his excitement and checked out the rest of the place. He noted a nice-sized kitchen tucked away behind the living room then focused his attention back to the unusual Christmas tree, decorated with glistening white miniature lights. He smiled at the silver icicles dangling from the blue spruce branches, as well as the penis-shaped candy canes, gingerbread men and women with intimate iced areas and large chocolate breasts, pussies and cocks. Sealed condoms in see-through wrappers and several tubes of lube also hung on the tree, and perched at the top of the tree were a pair of silver metal handcuffs.

Hmm, he could think of a few things he could do with those cuffs.

Connor's gaze wandered to the nearby stone fireplace. In its hearth a cheerful fire flickered, and hanging from the wood-beamed mantel were two huge red Christmas stockings, one in the shape of a cock, the other shaped like a breast.

Cute. His-and-hers erotic stockings. This place looked perfect for a sexfest getaway.

Dropping the luggage onto the couch, he shrugged out of his jacket, sweater and boots and headed for the fire. He'd just gotten himself warmed up when he heard a door closing from the loft area.

Softly padded footsteps followed. His heart settled into an excited pace and his head snapped up just in time to see a woman coming down the stairs toweling a mass dark-brown hair with a white towel. Her face was turned slightly away but she looked so damned familiar a shot of wicked arousal steamed through his balls and right up his shaft making him so fucking hard and horny he almost groaned out loud at the lightning-fast reaction.

Shit! These KF guys were good. From what he could see of the chick, she was a freaking Nurse Sparks clone. She hadn't seen him yet and he opted to remain silent as she strolled down the wood stairs.

She was wrapped in a sexy Santa-style bright-red mesh bathrobe. It hung wide open giving him a delicious glimpse of long feminine legs, a thonged pussy, a slightly rounded abdomen and the inside curves of a pair of generously sized breasts.

At the sight of seeing his first semi-naked woman in months, his breath literally stilled and his cock pulsed in sinful anticipation.

A moment later their gazes clashed and he started at the very familiar brown eyes that instantly twinkled in recognition.

"Nurse Sparks?"

"Sergeant Jordan?"

They spoke at the same time.

"What are you doing here?" Again, they spoke at the same time.

Connor found himself laughing. She smiled shyly and he didn't miss the pretty pink blush sweep across her cheeks.

As if stunned by his appearance, she remained on the stairs blinking at him, her Cupid-shaped mouth slightly open in an "O".

Was she disappointed in finding him there? What was she doing here? Had Kidnap Fantasies gone so far as to actually kidnap his nurse for him? And if that were the case, could he let her go if she wanted to leave?

Confusion mixed with excitement at actually seeing the woman who'd so tenderly cared for him during his stay at the hospital. The woman who, for some reason, had taken over his fantasy life ever since he'd met her.

"How have you been?" she asked softly.

"Been hanging okay. How about you?"

She shrugged her shoulders. "Lots of work and no play."

Lots of work and no play. He'd have to change that. And he'd have to change that starting right now.

Chapter Three

Tania couldn't believe the handsome soldier who'd been haunting her sexual fantasies actually stood right there in front of the cheerful fireplace. The intense way he looked at her made her feel as if she were a tasty morsel he wanted to devour.

How had this happened?

When she'd put in a request for a Kidnap Fantasies assignment for the holiday weekend centering around a man fitting the sergeant's physical description, she'd never thought in a million years that the original soldier would show up.

What the hell was Kidnap Fantasies doing? They knew she'd never mix her personal or professional life with her job as a KF employee.

Her face grew hotter. Did Connor know why she was really there?

"You didn't answer my question. Why are you here?" he asked as he walked toward her. Despite a slight limp he moved like a predatory animal. A man who'd finally captured his woman and wanted to brand her, claim her as his.

He moved cautiously so as not to spook her, yet confidently as if he knew what he wanted. And she knew he wanted her.

Had known it the instant his pain-filled green eyes had fluttered open in that hospital bed and he'd looked at her for the very first time. The heat in her cheeks began to spread, turning into something sensual as it quickly smoothed over her flesh. She could literally feel her breasts tightening, swelling in anticipation. Could feel her pussy heating, creaming, preparing for him.

She remained still as he came up the stairs toward her. Her mind churned with warnings against getting it on with a soldier. A man who, after he fully recuperated, would probably go back into the service and maybe get himself killed the next time around.

23

She shoved the disturbing thoughts aside as his masculine scent swept in all around her. He smelled so good. A combination of fresh air, spicy aftershave and his own unique sexy male scent.

He stopped a couple of steps below her. His warm breath splashed against her breasts and she suddenly remembered she'd left the robe open. She'd been expecting a customer, but not him. Not her sexy soldier.

Oh, God! What must he be thinking about her being there purely for sex?

"I've been thinking a lot about you, Florence," he said softly as he used his nickname for her. "Been remembering the intimate way you held my cock during the sponge baths you gave me."

Oh, my God!

"I've been fantasizing about you too," she whispered.

"You have?"

He sounded surprised. Obviously, she'd done a very good job in keeping her true feelings to herself...except for those sponge baths.

His gaze drew down from her face and settled on her heaving breasts. Arousal rumbled through her at his dark, hungry look.

"Obviously you're here because you want to be."

She nodded.

Wicked sensations shot through her as his hands lifted. His warm fingers touched her shoulders and he widened the front of her Santa Claus robe, exposing her full breasts.

He swore softly.

Her pussy creamed hard as his eyes wandered over every inch of her curves. He moved his head closer, the heat of his breath scorching the valley. One of his fingers gently stroked a hot, pink nipple. It beaded immediately. He fondled her there and the sensation of a rough callus on his finger scraped against her tender flesh making her tremble. Made her reach out and touch his cheek. It felt bristly from the stubble of his five o'clock shadow.

They stood that way. He, caressing her nipple. She, stroking his cheek. Both stared into each other's eyes, sending silent messages of what they needed. What they wanted.

His head bent closer and she cried out as his hot mouth enveloped her aching nipple. Sparks from his whiskers needled into her flesh. Lips tugged and pulled at her buds causing her pussy to contract.

Oh yes!

This was how she imagined her soldier to be. Rough, yet careful at the same time.

A warm hand pressed against her lower belly, branding her skin with an intense heat unlike anything she'd ever experienced. He sucked harder, sending sinful sensations spiraling through her.

Oh, God! She must be mad doing this.

Spearing her hands through his hair, she pulled his head into the cushion of her breast. She cradled him there and watched in whimpering fascination as his full lips suckled her nipple.

His hand moved from her abdomen, his long, masculine fingers sliding beneath her thong. She couldn't stop the inhalation of breath as a finger massaged her engorged clit. His intimate touch smoothed against her aching flesh with such a wondrous pressure she couldn't stop herself from grinding her hips against his hand.

When a finger slid inside her, her world tilted wonderfully. She moaned as a second finger invaded her sweet channel.

"You're dripping," he whispered as he let go of her nipple with a pop and grinned up at her.

"I'm horny," she admitted, loving the tiny wrinkles that appeared at the side of his eyes as he smiled.

"I think I can rectify that problem."

She squirmed as a third finger entered her. He pressed against her G-spot and she widened her legs.

"How does this make you feel, Florence?" he whispered.

Her mouth opened but no sound came out as he wiggled his fingers, creating a deeper friction.

"Feels good, doesn't it? I've waited so long to see this look on your face."

She could barely hear him, but she did notice the amusement in his voice. The lust. The satisfaction of finally having her.

A fourth digit impaled her. Arousal streaked up her pussy as he began a slow, erotic thrust. She could hear the slurping of her juices. Could smell her arousal. Could feel the pleasure squeezing through her cunt.

She tightened her grip on both sides of his head.

It felt so good having them inside her.

"But before I fuck you…"

"Oh, God!" she cried out as his fingers slipped out of her. She almost fell from the sudden, harsh abandonment. But he came up the two steps and suddenly they were face to face. Hot hands slid inside her open Santa robe. She whimpered as he held her hips. He pulled her close against his muscular body.

Then he looked up. "We're standing under the mistletoe."

She followed his gaze and couldn't believe she hadn't noticed the mistletoe when she'd arrived.

When she looked down again, he captured her mouth. He tasted heavenly as his firm lips moved over hers. The sliding sensation caused all the nerve endings in her body to sparkle. Her senses reeled.

She was losing control. Melting into a wonderful abyss of anticipation as he pressed his hard shaft so sweetly between her legs. When his tongue entered her mouth, Tania's world tilted and moaned.

"Do you feel my cock, Florence?" he said when he pulled his mouth away and breathed against her face. "That's what I've been living with while we've been apart. Now I'm going to show you what you've been missing. Do you want me inside you, Nurse Sparks?"

"Yes," she whispered without the slightest hesitation.

Burning fingers settled against the lapels of her Santa robe. Slowly, ever so slowly, he eased the delicate red material down over her shoulders. The garment dropped and pooled at her bare feet.

She stood naked in front of him. Naked except for the tiniest thong that protected her from the massive erection pressing against his pants.

"You shouldn't have held my cock so tenderly during those sponge baths, Nurse Sparks. Your touch gave me delicious ideas. A wicked arousal I just can't deny any longer."

His head lowered and his long tongue flicked against the tip of her hardened nipple and his mouth covered part of her breast.

Sweet Jesus! His lips were so hot on her flesh. Hot and intoxicating as he sucked on her other tight nipple. The sensation sent a waterfall of pleasure coursing through her. Sensations that made her ache with a need so powerful it left her dazed. Dazed and dripping with wetness between her legs.

Need raged inside her. Desperate cravings tumbled together and snowballed into an exquisite want to be satisfied by her sexy soldier.

Too hell with protocol. Here, she wasn't a professional. Here, she was a woman who needed to be satisfied.

She wanted him to plunge the thick, heavy rod deep inside her. Yet at the same time, she needed his mouth kissing every intimate curve of her trembling body. Her heart pounded violently as he let go of her nipple and pulled her thong down over her wide hips exposing her nude pussy to his wanton gaze.

A wonderfully confident thumb slammed against her already ultra-sensitive clit, making her cry out from the intense arousal.

She felt feverish. The mesmerizing combination of his thumb grazing her clit and his firm lips that were now back to suckling on her nipple sent a disturbing wave of impatience ripping through her.

"Connor," she whimpered. "Please."

She cried out as his four fingers once again slid back into her wet channel. He pumped her so fucking hard she climaxed almost immediately.

She shook at the intensity of it.

Waves of pleasure gripped her. His fingers continued to fuck her in long, steady strokes. The pleasure screamed through her vagina, roared through her body and she cried out Connor's name over and over again.

Suddenly his fingers left her and he was leading her up the stairs. Up to the loft with the cozy king-size brass bed covered in delicious fluffy comforters.

But he didn't take her to the bed. Instead, he led her to the shaggy, grizzly bearskin rug lying on the wood-planked floor in front of the upstairs fireplace. A cheerful fire roared in the hearth, compliments of the wood she'd tossed in after coming out of the hot tub and before she'd showered.

"Get onto your hands and knees. I want to take you from behind," he whispered.

From behind! Like the predatory animal she'd sensed he'd be. The rug felt warm beneath her hands and knees as she got into the doggie-style position.

"But what about your injuries? Are you well enough?"

"I'll deal with it." He swore softly. "When did you put that plug in?"

"This morning."

"I'll have to wait a little longer before taking that sweet ass of yours. I want you nice and stretched for me."

Her pulses pounded. Exactly how big was he when fully erect?

"Just keep your eyes on the flames, Nurse Tania. And brace yourself." She trembled at his lust-filled voice. Whimpered as she saw a distorted view of his reflection in the glass shield in front of the fire. She watched as he quickly unbuttoned his shirt. Her heart hammered at the sound of his zipper lowering, the rustle of clothing being removed.

The sound of plastic ripping. A condom. *Be prepared.* The motto of Kidnap Fantasies.

She could tell he was naked. Gloriously naked. Before she could turn around to see how he'd look, his large, smooth cock head slid against her already sensitized clit. He massaged her until she was once again moaning and desperate for him. Until her pussy quivered for him.

Warm hands slid against her waist. His fingers dug into her flesh as he held her still, readied her for his impalement.

One quick, hard thrust and his huge member sank into her vagina. His thickness stretched her and her vaginal muscles contracted wildly around him as she welcomed him inside.

"So tight," he groaned.

"Deeper," she moaned, loving the velvety feel of his hard rod traveling into her tender pussy.

He pushed harder, deeper, until swollen testicles were pressed intimately against her ass. The agonizing pressure of his cock buried inside her increased her own pleasure. She bucked her hips against him and smiled at his guttural groans.

He began to thrust. Strong, pistoning motions that burned her with pleasure.

He moved faster. Deeper. In and out.

Slurping sounds filled the air and in moments a fire ripped through her. She convulsed wildly. Cried out his name as she came, her muscles gripping him tightly.

He continued to thrust, increasing the driving pleasure.

He groaned. His flesh tightened inside her.

Then he came, crying out as he joined her in orgasm.

Chapter Four

Wow. That was fucking beautiful, Connor thought a few minutes later. Warm air blew against his face from the nearby fireplace as both of them lay on the rug, their breaths harsh and fast from the lovemaking session.

He had Tania cocooned in front of him, her flesh wickedly hot as he spooned himself against her soft, feminine curves. His cock, still buried deep inside her, pulsed in answer to the tiny after-contractions of her orgasm.

He lay in such a way that allowed her to use his outstretched arm as a pillow, and with his free hand he gently explored one of her firm breasts.

"I've missed you," she whispered.

"You mean you missed the sponge baths," he chuckled.

She shook her head. "No, I mean I've wanted this. I've wanted what happened tonight. I've wanted it from the moment I saw you."

Fuck! "You did a fine job in hiding your feelings, Florence."

She tightened against his nickname for her.

"Please, don't call me that anymore."

"Why not?" He thought she'd liked being nicknamed after the famous woman who'd pioneered modern nursing.

"Because it reminds me of the Florence Nightingale Syndrome."

Shit! He'd used the same excuse for forcing himself not to get involved with her. For denying the attraction he felt for her.

"About how soldiers fall in love with their nurses?"

"Yes."

He'd heard about it. Heard about the high failure rate of those relationships. It was the reason he'd kept his distance from her, despite the overwhelming urge to be with her.

"So you think what we feel for each other is serious?"

"I...I don't know. We hardly know each other," she said quietly.

30

"I'd say the sexual attraction that's been between us since day one, those luscious sponge baths that left me so fucking hard for you, and now tonight is something we can start a relationship on, don't you?"

He held his breath awaiting her answer.

"I...feel guilty."

"Why?"

"Because...I'm a professional nurse. You were my patient and the thoughts I have for you are so...unprofessional."

"I like the sound of that."

She giggled and he gently squeezed her nipple.

"I just can't believe I've done this," she said.

To his surprise she intertwined her fingers with the hand he had outstretched in front of her. He looked down and smiled. Such an intimate gesture from someone he barely knew.

"Save that kind of talk for the morning after, Tania. I've got all night to fuck that guilt right out of you. By morning, you'll have changed your mind."

"Promise?"

"Cross my heart."

* * * * *

Tania smiled the next afternoon while she lay in bed with Connor, all her guilt gone, as they stared at the snowdrifts hugging the glass panes. Sometime during the night it had stopped snowing and now a bright sunshine streamed though the windows allowing them to see the snow-capped mountains on the other side of the valley.

She'd never felt so relaxed after a full night of sex. They'd made love, played in the hot tub on the balcony. Made love again. He'd brought her to orgasm after orgasm after orgasm. He'd even served her breakfast in bed before fucking her again.

Now as they lay in bed resting after yet another lovemaking session, she couldn't stop herself from sliding her hand behind her. He moaned when she wound her fingers around his pulsing cock. She could never get enough of touching him. His rod was so hot, deliciously thick and so blessedly long in her hand.

"Be prepared to take the consequences for handling the merchandise," he teased against her ear.

Her tummy suddenly hollowed out in despair. *Be prepared.* Kidnap Fantasies motto. It was time to tell him the truth about herself.

"Connor, I think before this goes any further...I should tell you something. Something you might not like."

"Whatever you tell me I'll like...unless you're suddenly married," he chuckled.

"No. I'm too busy to be married." She'd never thought about marriage with any other man. *Until now.*

"I..." Oh hell, she might as well just say it. But it was just so damned hard. She didn't want him to think of her as being bad for doing what she did to alleviate her stress. She wanted him to think of her as Florence, a woman dedicated to her job. But she also loved to play.

"My job burned me out a couple of times. In order to avoid it again, I picked up a hobby."

"Hobbies are good."

As if sensing her turmoil he moved closer against her. Snuggled a warm hand between her legs and gently cupped her pussy.

"You aren't making this easy, soldier."

He chuckled, and she inhaled sharply as he pressed the palm of his hand against her clit.

"Just spill it, Tania. Nothing you say will turn me off to you. I've been fucking you all night and all morning, and I just keep wanting more and more of you."

Sweet heavens. She felt the same way about him.

"Okay...so, um...I occasionally work for Kidnap Fantasies. I had no idea you would be my client."

The hand against her pussy stilled. Ouch! Her confession had hurt him.

She continued. "And I enjoy being kidnapped. It's an adrenaline rush for me. It makes me horny. It makes it easier for me to have sex with the strange men...or women I've been assigned to."

To her surprise, he chuckled. "Seeing you horny makes me horny."

"You're not upset?"

"No fucking way. And to prove it..." He tossed aside the sheets covering him, giving her a glimpse of his scarred legs before he stood and padded over to her side of the bed.

Goodness! She couldn't believe how easily he'd just accepted she was an employee of Kidnap Fantasies and that she'd admitted she had a kidnap fetish. She'd never told any of her previous boyfriends. Nor any of her sisters.

Connor just didn't seem to care that she'd entertained other men and women in this same way. Obviously, he was prepared to take her any way he could get her. But was it just for this holiday weekend? Or did he want her forever, as she wanted him?

Her pussy creamed at the lusty look in his green eyes. Her lower belly clenched at the hard, pulsing cock protruding from the nest of pubic hair.

"I can see you're all ready for some more action," she teased.

"As you've probably already noticed, Tania. I'm always ready for you."

Oh baby! She'd noticed.

Coming around to her side of the bed, he pushed the cozy comforters aside allowing the cool air in the bedroom to splash over her nakedness.

"It's cold!" she cried out. They'd been so busy fucking they hadn't set the fires in the fireplaces or turned up the heat. She tried to scramble away onto his side of the bed, to dive under the covers, but he caught her around the waist. He easily picked her up.

"We'll generate our own heat," he growled as he carried her into the bathroom.

"Please let me down. You'll hurt yourself. Your legs—"

"I'll hurt more if I don't fuck you now," he complained as he set her down on her feet just outside the shower. As if sensing she would try to escape and head back for the warmth of the bed, he kept a strong muscular arm anchored around her waist as he adjusted the water taps.

A moment later, he swept her off her feet and settled her in a standing position in the deep bathtub. He quickly positioned her in front of the showerhead and she cried out as lusciously hot water slammed onto her tender breasts.

"Raise your arms behind your head. Keep them there. I'm going to remove the butt plug."

She didn't even hesitate to follow his strangled order. Clasping her hands behind her neck, her breath halted in her throat as needle pricks of pressure slammed without mercy onto her breasts. She watched her nipples blush and felt the butt plug move ever so slowly out of her.

"Hold on a sec. Have to lube." He grabbed the tube of lube hanging on the showerhead.

While she waited for him fear zipped through her arousal as a thought struck her. Connor's erection was so big. So thick.

Would he fit inside her ass?

Her fear turned into arousal again as a moment later his lubed flesh suddenly pushed between her ass cheeks against her anal hole. He pressed hard and a moment later, he passed through her sphincter muscle.

Oh boy, he certainly was big.

He stretched her ass sweetly. A pleasure burn burst through her. She moaned at the sensual impact. Her hands clasped harder against the back of her neck. She gritted her teeth and held herself still. When he'd buried his entire shaft deep inside her, she could barely breathe from her excitement. She cried out as his hot hands gripped her hips. His fingers dug into her flesh as he began to pump. Deep, hard thrusts.

Her nipples elongated. Turned a pretty pink. Hardened into tight beads.

He continued to thrust. Her pussy creamed, her breath was coming so fast.

She closed her eyes. Fought for control. Pleasure gripped her as he continued to thrust into her ass.

During her years with Kidnap Fantasies, she'd been trained at their various sex camps to orgasm with anal penetration. Now she could feel her climax blossoming like wildfire. It threatened to consume her.

She could feel his body tightening against her back as he thrust inside her and she knew he was just as close to climaxing as she was.

"Brace yourself," he said.

To her surprise, his hands left her waist and came around to cup her breasts.

She moaned at the impact of his heat slicing into her skin. Her mind screamed for mercy as his fingers erotically massaged her mounds. He pulled her nipples. Twisted them, plucked at them until pleasure-pain burned and she cried out.

"You respond so passionately," he said softly against her ear. She could barely hear him above the splash of the shower.

His hands left her breasts. One nestled on her lower abdomen just above her pussy. He held her there, keeping her steady so he could continue pumping into her.

When a long, callused finger slid over her clit, she groaned and fought back her need for release.

"You want to come, don't you?"

"Yes." Oh yes! She was ready to come.

She hissed as he kissed the sensitive area behind her right ear.

"Don't come. Not without my permission," he whispered. He continued to massage her clit as he furiously pumped into her.

God! He was torturing her!

Her lower belly clenched. Her anal muscles tightened around his flesh. She couldn't stop herself from moaning at the overwhelming need to climax.

"Jesus! Let me come, Connor."

"Can't you handle some more, Tania?"

"No," she gasped.

"Neither can I. You can come now."

And did she ever. She virtually exploded and shivered uncontrollably as bolts of pleasure tangled through her mind, body and soul.

Exotic waves screamed through her. Her pussy clenched. She cried out as he slipped three fingers inside her soaked vagina and pumped her hard and fast.

Pleasure unlike anything she'd ever known tore her apart. She could barely hear his groans. Could barely feel the last three hard thrusts into her tender ass or the warm jets of sperm filling her.

Afterward he carried her into the loft and she smiled. It was such a pretty place with cute flowered wallpaper, the cranberry, white and turquoise color scheme. Soft flannel sheets snuggled against the bottom of her body as he laid her out on the bed. He slipped in beside her. She snuggled beside the man she barely knew and felt so content. When he pulled the fluffy, warm, feather comforters over her, she was already asleep.

Chapter Five

It was a strangled cry from Connor that woke Tania and sent a rush of concern screaming through her. For a moment, she felt disoriented in the darkness, and suddenly remembered they'd made love all day with small breaks for food and fun in the hot tub.

Night had descended once again and they'd fallen asleep.

Another cry from him made her fumble for the lamp beside the bed. She flicked the light on and what she saw alarmed her.

Connor lay in bed, the comforters kicked away by his scarred feet, his face white and drenched in a glistening sweat.

"Connor," she whispered, knowing she had to be careful around soldiers and their nightmares. Knew it was a common occurrence during the months after the physical recuperation as the mind tried to sort out what had happened to the body.

"Connor," she said again, a little louder this time.

His eyes snapped open. For a moment they were glazed with fear, then recognition flooded them.

"Florence?"

Tania smiled in relief. "Welcome back, soldier."

"What's wrong?"

"You were having a nightmare. Do you want to talk about it?"

She already knew what had happened to him. It was the same story from the wounded men being shipped back home with missing body parts, nervous disorders, shrapnel wounds—the list went on and on.

Connor had been in serious condition when he'd first been put into her care. She'd read in the medical files accompanying him that he'd died twice on the table when they'd been extracting a shard of shrapnel from near his heart. Like most soldiers, he relived what he'd endured through regular nightmares.

He said nothing and stared straight up at the ceiling.

"Talking does help."

"I've talked with the shrinks. They didn't help."

"You never talked with me."

He grimaced. "I don't want to lay this shit on you, Tania."

"It's not shit, soldier. They're your feelings. Raw and wild emotions that need to be soothed."

"You can soothe me in other ways," he said softly. He closed his eyes but she could read the anguish on his face.

"I'll soothe you if you open up to me, Connor. Tell me what happened that day in Iraq."

"You're so pure and innocent. I don't want to ruin you with my memories."

Tania couldn't help but laugh. She slapped a hand against her naked chest in mock horror, the sound of it making him open his eyes to look at her.

"Me? Pure and innocent? Hello. I told you I work for Kidnap Fantasies. I'm also a nurse. I am anything but pure or innocent. Lay your shit on me anytime, soldier."

"Blackmail."

"No, it's called concern for you. You need to talk it out, or you'll explode."

"Nothing that your tight little pussy won't cure. Or your cute ass," he grinned.

"No games, Connor. I'm serious. You need to let the poison out."

He swallowed and his Adam's apple bobbed wildly. She frowned and swirled a finger around the round, puckered flesh near his heart where a piece of near-deadly shrapnel had knifed into him.

"Okay, I'll tell you."

Thank God.

"We'd been sent on a mission. Needed to get fuel to some of our men stationed in a remote area of Iraq. Men who'd cornered some insurgents. I was in the Humvee behind the fuel tanker. Exposed as I sat on the turret, manning the machine gun. I was keeping an eye out, scanning the surrounding desert for any sign of trouble." He hesitated. Frowned. "Suddenly there was this huge bang. An orange ball went up right in front of me. Before I knew what was happening I was thrown through the air like a rag doll. I hit the sand hard. It knocked the breath out of me. Scared the shit out of me."

She could see him trembling beside her and she pressed her hand over the area of his heart and willed for it to slow down.

It didn't.

"After the explosion, it literally rained metal. One piece got me in the chest. I couldn't see it. My eyes were blurry. Burned from the explosion. But I felt it going in like a sharp twist of a knife. Another piece of metal, a huge one, came down on both my legs. It pinned me. Burned into me. And, as you know, it broke the bones in my lower legs. I could barely feel any pain after that, until later."

Shock.

"And you felt helpless. Afraid."

He nodded. "But not afraid for me. For my buddies. I could hear their screams. I wanted to get to them. Couldn't fucking move. Couldn't fucking see."

He shuddered.

Tania continued to stroke his chest, tracing a pebbled nipple, wondering if touching him so intimately was the right thing to do. She hoped her touches would anchor him. Would keep him grounded in knowing he could trust her into soothing his pain.

Maybe even anchor her from starting to cry at what Connor and the other soldiers must have gone through and were still going through in Iraq.

"I could smell their flesh burning. Could hear their screams. I couldn't get to them."

"But how could you? It isn't your fault. You were pinned."

"I just wanted to help them." His tortured voice ripped a hole into her heart. Moisture blurred her vision.

"I started screaming for someone to get the metal off my legs. I could hear them suffering all around me and then, after a while, there was silence, ice-cold silence in the middle of a hot desert...shit. A survivor managed to get the metal off me before collapsing. He and I were the only ones who made it out alive that day." The guilt in his voice made a sick heaviness settle in her tummy. She nestled into the crook of his strong arms and she wrapped her arm across his waist, holding him tight to her. He held her firmly too, as if she were the one who needed comforting and not him.

She, who needed to remain strong for all her wounded soldiers, suddenly felt lost and helpless in the arms of a man she'd thought she'd never get involved with. Now lying there in his arms, she knew it wouldn't be easy for him to let his memories go, just as she knew it wouldn't be easy for her to ever let him go.

*****

They lay together wrapped in each other's arms for a long time before the harsh memories slowly ebbed and the trembling in his limbs finally subsided.

She was the anchor he needed in his life now. A sexy nurse who he'd fallen in love with over and over again so many times in the hospital and again here. Every time he gazed upon her, his heart simply overflowed with love. He doubted he'd survive if she decided their time together in the chalet was just part of her job.

"I don't know much about you, Nurse Sparks. You always kept your family life hidden. Tell me a little bit about yourself," he whispered as he watched her breasts rise and fall with her every breath.

"Hmm, what do you want to know?"

"Where were you born? Where's your family? Any boyfriends?"

"Boyfriends? Lots of them."

His gut twisted. She'd had many men while working at Kidnap Fantasies.

"Sorry, I guess that was insensitive of me."

He squeezed her closer to him, loving the heat of her against his flesh.

"No, baby. You can tell me anything. I'll never judge."

"You're too good to be true, Connor."

"That's the same way I feel about you too."

She tilted her head back a little and gazed up at him. Her eyes looked so brown and deep he felt as if he were falling into a pool of chocolate.

"Well, I was born and raised an Army brat. I have three sisters, all younger than me. As I was growing up we moved around so many times that I'm surprised I don't have multiple personality syndrome because I tended to take on a new identity with every place we moved to... I guess you could call me a free spirit. My mom and dad told me if I'd been born into any other family, I probably would have pursued an acting career. Instead I went into nursing."

"And then Kidnap Fantasies. How did you get into KF?"

"Through a friend. She suggested it after my second burnout."

"You always looked so refreshed and happy when you were tending to us in the hospital."

"Actress mode." She frowned. "Seriously though. It's hard to watch the wounded men and women suffer. Hard to see how their lives have been changed by war. We all have to find ways to keep our patients' spirits up, y'know. They need us to take care of them. They need us to be positive for them. To help them get back on track. And we can't do it if we don't find outlets. I deal with the stress by getting myself kidnapped and taking on occasional assignments with Kidnap Fantasies. It's extreme, but it works for me."

"Can't hold it against a girl for trying to keep her sanity," Connor said, and pressed his lips to her warm, velvety forehead.

"Just as I can't hold it against a guy for hiring Kidnap Fantasies. So, why did you?"

"It was a gift from my brothers to get you out of my system."

"Really?"

"Yes, really. I couldn't get you out of my head after leaving the hospital."

She cocked a perfectly arched eyebrow at him. "Why not just come and pursue me?"

"The Florence Nightingale Syndrome."

"Oh my gosh, why didn't you tell me that was your excuse when we talked about it earlier?"

"I had other things on my mind," he chuckled, and kissed her cute button nose. "Just as I have other things on my mind right now other than talking."

She giggled again. Those giggles quickly turned to aroused whimpers as he clamped his mouth over hers in a fierce kiss.

* * * * *

Christmas Eve

Early the next morning they made love again, this time under the Christmas tree. Then they made love on the kitchen table after breakfast.

And then Santana showed up.

Santana, who worked for Kidnap Fantasies.

Tania'd been fucked by him on several occasions when she'd needed a third. He was a big, sexy, bi black man who totally enjoyed pleasuring both sexes in a ménage.

After getting Connor and Santana reacquainted downstairs in front of a roaring fire in the hearth, she'd discreetly made herself scarce by going up to the loft to shower.

Santana was very good at his job, and he'd ease Connor into his sexual fantasy without Connor getting nervous. Well, at least not too nervous.

Last night, he'd confessed to her he was uneasy about getting together with a man. But she'd reassured him a large percentage of men occasionally fantasized about doing it with the same sex. If the urge were great, some men acted on it. The butt plug she'd inserted into his cute ass would make it easier for him.

And it looked as though they hadn't wasted any time as Tania noticed when, wrapped in a towel, she came out of the upstairs bathroom and entered the loft to the sounds of aroused masculine groans coming from downstairs. Her heart picked up a mad pace as she tiptoed to the railing and looked down into the living room.

Both men were beautifully naked. White and black muscles glistened as the bright wintry sunshine splashed over them from the various arched windows.

Connor's face was clenched in erotic bliss as his engorged shaft slid in and out of Santana's eagerly sucking mouth.

Her body tightened as she watched them. Before she knew what she was doing, her finger had slipped beneath her towel and she'd begun a mad massage against her ultra-sensitive clit.

* * * * *

Connor's breaths came hard and fast as he watched his penis drive in and out of Santana's mouth. The black man's lips were firm and moist, clenching around his flesh like a woman's tight pussy. Santana's eyes were closed tightly, his nostrils flared and he had a serene look on his face as if he truly enjoyed sucking on a man's cock.

Fuck! It was amazing how fast things had happened. One minute he and Tania had taken a break from their sexfest and been roasting marshmallows in the fireplace. The next minute Santana, the easygoing Kidnap Fantasies man who'd picked him up from the airport, had shown up with an armful of Christmas presents for them.

After placing the presents under the tree, Santana had started small talk with both Tania and him. It had led to jokes that had put Connor immediately at ease.

He knew why Santana was there. In the Kidnap Fantasies questionnaire, Connor had written down he wanted to try a sex-with-a-man fantasy. He'd known Santana would be the one when they'd talked about it in the car on the way from the airport.

After Tania had excused herself to go for a shower, Connor had noticed the black man's eyes darken with lust.

And to Connor's surprise, he'd responded.

Santana was a strikingly handsome man. Very tall. Short, black curly hair. Clean shaven. Wide shoulders with smooth, chocolate-colored skin. He looked similar to Denzel Washington, the movie star, and Connor realized Kidnap Fantasies had probably hired him for that reason.

But not for that reason alone.

The man was good at his job because Connor had felt so at ease in his presence, he'd been surprised when he responded so naturally to Santana's heated look.

His balls had tightened with need and his cock had stirred with arousal. Santana, sensing Connor's reaction, had suddenly leaned in closer and touched his warm lips to his.

It felt different kissing a man instead of a woman. With a woman, he felt a need to push, to dominate. With a man...his equal...he felt challenged.

But in a good way.

Their kiss had led to intimate touches.

Then Santana's hand had slipped into Connor's track pants. He'd begun a slow massage on Connor's balls. A nice hard rub with rough twists to his scrotum, making his breath quicken and weird little moans escape his mouth. Santana's touches had unleashed wickedly carnal sensations making Connor's lower belly clench and lightning blades of lust slam through him.

Before he'd known it, Santana had seduced him right out of his pants. The black man, suddenly naked, had gotten onto his knees before him and taken Connor's engorged erection into his hot, moist mouth.

To Connor's surprise, he didn't feel the least bit embarrassed. Santana was obviously a man who put his clients at ease with his easygoing, soft-spoken nature.

The black man's full lips felt fantastic wrapped firmly around his cock. The pull of his mouth, the strong sucking motions, the teasing way his tongue caressed the underneath skin of his shaft made Connor so hard so fast the pressure had him calling out his warning.

"Jesus. I'm ready to come."

He groaned when Santana pulled his mouth away with a pop, leaving him so hard and so ready to come he almost fell to his knees, his legs were trembling so badly.

"On your hands and knees," the big black man ordered. "I need to fuck your ass, man."

Connor's breaths came in excited gasps as he eagerly did what Santana instructed.

Shit! He couldn't believe a man had just been sucking on him. It had felt fantastic. He wanted more from Santana. *Much* more.

Looking over his shoulder, he watched with a wild anticipation as Santana's arms bulged with nicely shaped muscles as he grabbed a condom dangling off a nearby branch on the Christmas tree, tore open the foil and sheathed himself with it. Then he located a tube of lube hanging from another branch and began to generously lube his shaft. A hell of a big member that was firm and erect. Connor had been right. The man had gotten turned-on big-time sucking him.

He couldn't help but compare their sizes.

Santana's cock was bigger than his own. Thicker, maybe three inches wide. Longer than his shaft. Definitely longer. At least ten inches of pulsing vein-riddled flesh with a large satiny black mushroom-shaped cock head.

Connor swallowed at the sudden tightness in his throat and wondered how his virgin ass could accommodate such a length and thickness.

He couldn't help but tense in wicked anticipation when Santana came toward him with big, lubed cock in his hand, an aroused grin on his face.

"I've been wanting to fuck you since I saw you at the airport," he whispered.

Connor's heart began a wild beat at Santana's admission.

"Brace yourself, man. Brace yourself for one wicked ride, Connor."

Connor flinched as his ass cheeks were spread wide and inhaled sharply as Santana slowly removed the butt plug. A second later, his cock head probed gently at the tight entrance to his hole.

"I have a fetish for virgin asses," Santana breathed. "They turn me on so fucking much I can barely keep my control."

His hot penis began an insistent probing. Connor exhaled his growing tension.

"Easy, man." Santana soothed as he pressed past his sphincter muscle and tunneled into his ass.

"Don't worry. Just relax."

Connor groaned at the pleasure-burn fullness stretching into him.

"It'll be great, man. You'll see. You're going to love it. Crave it. Need it."

Jesus. He already craved it.

Santana's lubed cock moved easily, gently, into him and before he knew it, he felt the black man's swollen testicles press against his own.

"Oh yeah, that feels fantastic," Santana groaned as he went still for a moment.

His solid erection pulsed inside Connor's ass and he loved the silky, unfamiliar full feeling of being impaled. His own desire grew as his anal muscles eagerly clenched the intruder.

Then Santana began fucking him.

Starting with a slow, steady rhythm and building quickly into dark, carnal plunges. The solid length of the man's shaft drove harder, faster. With every thrust his own cock pulsed as Santana's rod pressed against his sensitive prostate gland.

Shit! He could feel his balls tightening. Could feel the blood engorging up his swollen shaft. The impending pleasure threatening to consume him any second.

He cried out as Tania's hot hand clasped his rod. She was there. Naked. On her hands and knees beside him while Santana fucked his ass.

She smiled teasingly as she reached out. Her fingers clutched him, twisted his shaft until Connor was perspiring and shaking so hard with arousal he thought he would simply explode. Her other hand expertly massaged his balls until he was gasping out for mercy.

His breath caught as she lay down on the carpet and wiggled beneath him and splayed herself out like a luscious offering.

"Fuck her, Connor. Fuck her while I fuck you," Santana groaned.

Wow.

"I'm so ready, Connor. So horny watching you two," Tania said softly.

His breath ripped from his mouth as her fingers wrapped tightly around his pulsing cock. She was pulling at him. Pulling him down.

Santana's engorged cock stilled in Connor's ass, allowing him to spread his knees onto each side of Tania's hips. He hissed as a zip of pain ripped through one of his injured legs in the awkward position. He ignored it.

They both cried out as Connor sank deep into her pussy. Her velvety muscles wrapped around him and welcomed him in. Her cunt felt so soft. So wet.

"Follow my moves, man," Santana ordered in a strangled voice. He started thrusting into his ass again. Connor immediately understood. Quickly, he found the black man's rhythm and moved with him. As he slid out of Tania's tight sheath, Santana slid out of his ass. As he plunged into Tania, Santana thrust into him.

Tania's eyes were closed tightly. Her cheeks flushed pink. Soft gasps escaped her slightly parted lips as he slammed into her and Santana into him.

Oh yeah, she liked it hard. He could tell by the way her vagina grabbed at his flesh and didn't want to let go.

He liked it too. Loved the way his cock hardened inside her. Loved the way Santana's penis was strengthening inside him. The fullness of the black man's flesh impaling him felt fantastic.

He groaned as spasms from her vagina embraced and squeezed his erection.

She was coming. Coming hard. Coming fast.

Her face twisted into a serene bliss and she cried out her release. Her plump breasts jiggled beneath him with their thrusts. It wasn't long before blades of arousal zipped through his lower belly and his entire body tensed.

Oh yeah!

"I'm coming," he hissed.

The explosion hit. It tore through his balls in jagged bolts. Shimmered up his cock like a bolt of lightning. He shuddered beneath the pleasure assault and he came inside Tania.

A moment later on a hoarse, guttural shout, the black man came inside him.

Chapter Six

"I need to get cleaned up," Santana groaned moments later after the three of them had separated. The black man winked at Tania and got up and walked into the nearby bathroom, as if to give them an intimate moment alone.

"How...how was it?" she breathed as the two of them sat facing each other on the carpet in front of the fireplace.

"It was fantastic. I've never felt so...high." His eyes were glazed, as if he were truly high, Tania noted. She was thrilled his first same-sex experience and ménage had worked out so well.

"Watching the two of you... I never thought I could be so turned-on."

Connor's gaze darkened and he suddenly helped her to her feet. "I want more."

She heard Santana coming out of the bathroom. Licked her lips as Connor's shaft hardened. Her heart crashed against her chest as another condom pack was ripped open. Then Santana came up behind her. She didn't have to be told the solid piece of heated flesh pressing against her bare ass was his rigid cock.

God! Santana was already rock-hard again!

"I've been dying to fuck you for so long," Santana whispered softly. He gently kissed the sensitive area between her neck and shoulder. His warm lips made her flesh tingle, made her want more of his kisses.

"Your skin feels so silky, Tania. Bring your arms behind your back for me."

Excitement roared through her. She couldn't move. She felt off balance at the wild lust splashed across Connor's face as he watched Santana pressing in behind her. His cheeks were flushed and the brilliant lust in his eyes made her body tighten with need.

Connor's thick shaft was once again stretched outward from his mat of curls. Below it, she spotted the two swollen egg-shaped spheres bulging against his sac. One hand was wrapped tightly around the base of his swollen erection and the fingers of his other hand stroked the pulsing blue vein that ran up his cock.

"Do as he says, Tania," he whispered.

Her lower belly clenched as she brought both her arms back, allowing her breasts to push out. Something cold and metallic snapped around her wrists and she heard the click of the handcuffs slamming home.

Her pussy throbbed with excitement. She was now their captive.

Her breathing became rougher as she followed Connor's gaze to her breasts. They heaved up and down with her every breath. Her nipples were elongating, flushing a bright red as blood pumped into them.

"Spread your legs for him, Tania," Connor whispered as he continued to stroke his shaft.

Taking a slow, shuddering breath she did as Connor said.

"I can already see the pleasure on your face, Tania," he whispered. "And it's turning me on big-time."

"She's beautiful. Absolute perfection," Santana whispered.

A deep, sinking sexual awareness churned in her lower belly as Santana crouched behind her, his dark knees came down on the plush carpet between her legs. A moment later his warm, moist lips slid over her right ass cheek in sweet, gentle kisses.

Her legs trembled at the delightful touches of a man's mouth on her ass and she thought her legs might give out.

Connor came closer. His fingertips brushed teasingly along the curve of her neck, over her collarbone and along the side curves of her breasts.

With her hands cuffed, she could do nothing but stand there as the two men explored and touched her intimately. Connor tweaked and pinched her nipples until they burned and her breasts felt wonderfully achy. Santana's velvety lips continued to slide over her ass cheeks with occasional nips from sharp teeth that made her ass blaze just as wickedly as her nipples.

Connor's hands came down and slid over her waist. The intense heat of his palms on her flesh made her cunt cream even more. Wetness dripped along the insides of her thighs. She cried out when Santana's hot tongue suddenly lapped against her sensitive clit.

She bucked violently.

Connor chuckled at her reaction and his hands slowly skimmed along her hips, brushing her flesh with featherlight touches that made her gyrate.

Santana's tongue swiped back and forth against her clit and she bucked again, spreading her legs wider.

"So fucking sweet," Santana murmured. "And already sopping wet. She's already ready for us."

His tongue speared into her pussy, hot and demanding, stroking the walls of Tania's vagina and pressing against her ultra-sensitive G-spot.

Perspiration popped out on her flesh as he pushed harder, rubbing and pressing her sensitive spot until the pressure turned into a deep, odd pleasure.

Wicked tremors coursed through her. She closed her eyes. Her body grew feverish with need. Her pussy felt hot. Heavy. Soaked.

She cried out as Santana's hot tongue left her dripping pussy. A moment later slurping sounds split the air as the big black man lubed his penis.

In front of her, Connor's heavy breaths ripped through the air. His hand guided his solid erection between her pussy lips and lodged at her tiny vaginal opening. His hands then resettled onto the curves of her full hips.

"Oh yes! Please, Connor. Fuck me." She was so hot now. So ready. She could barely keep her eyes open.

But she'd didn't have any problems opening them when moments later the giant mushroom-shaped lubed cock head pressed against her trembling little anal hole.

She whimpered, momentary fear intermingling with her arousal. She'd forgotten how big Santana's cock was.

"Shh, I'm here, baby," Connor said softly. He nodded at Santana and she could feel his thick flesh press eagerly against her tightly clenched anal ring. In a moment he pushed past and slipped into her ass.

Tania dug her fingers into her palms and her breath caught as Connor's penis sank slowly into her vagina. Her ring gave way and her anal muscles clenched around Santana's thick invasion.

She moaned. Pressure made her try to move away from them, but Connor's hands kept her firm.

"She's so goddamn tight," Santana panted.

Tania moaned as the two shafts burned into her.

Sweet heavens, she could feel every long inch moving inside her two channels! Pleasure-pain burned into her ass, making her grimace. Making her whimper over and over. Santana's hard, heated length bore into her like a thick piece of hot metal.

Connor's hot mouth melted over her quivering lips, trapping her moans. From somewhere far away, she could hear Santana's hoarse whisper, "I'm almost fully inside her. Just one more inch."

Her vagina creamed as Connor's thick cock head moved deeper into her. Unbelievable thickness powered into her.

Santana's hands came around to her front. He cupped her swollen breasts and held tight as he rammed his final inch into her.

She was now impaled on both men's cocks. Locked into them. Sandwiched between them, anxiously waiting for them to do to her whatever they wanted.

It made her want to scream at them to hurry. To hurry and make her fly with arousal. Every nerve ending was on fire. Her vaginal muscles quivered around Connor's cock. Her asshole blazed with Santana's thick rod.

Santana's hands were moving over her breasts now, tweaking her nipples.

The lower half of Connor was pushed into her belly. His pubic bones were grinding against hers and his swollen balls were pressing against her flesh.

Suddenly, Connor stopped kissing her.

"Open your eyes, Tania," he whispered.

She did as he asked. It was hard though. So hard to open her eyes.

"We're going to fuck you now, Tania. We're going to fuck you so hard you'll be screaming and begging us to never stop."

She gave a little excited cry at his words.

What she was experiencing so far from the double penetration—the pleasure-pain from two massive rods burning deep inside her—made her wonder how much carnal anguish she might be able to handle.

Her mind spiraled as both of the men slid their hard erections out of her.

She cried out as Connor thrust into her in one swift plunge. As he withdrew, Santana's huge shaft rammed into her ass.

Tania arched against them, not knowing whether to push her ass into the exquisite pleasure-pain Santana created or if she should press into Connor's wildly delicious plunges.

They continued to pump into her tight holes with an exquisite tempo.

They fucked her hard. Fast and furious. They used her viciously. Invaded her channels with their rigid shafts.

She writhed and bucked against them, eagerly accepting their heated thrusts. They made her come over and over again. Made her burn and shatter. Showered her with carnal pleasure-pain and exquisite joy. Her mind filled with nothing but ecstasy.

Their two cocks destroyed her.

Made her scream. Made her want more and more.

Perspiration drenched her and sexual exhaustion eventually took hold.

Finally they both ejaculated into her.

* * * * *

Christmas Day

Connor stared out the frost-laced window whistling beneath his breath as the bright Christmas morning sunshine peeked over the snowcapped mountains on the other side of the valley.

"Looks beautiful, doesn't it?" Tania said.

She stretched lazily in the bed where the two men had tucked her after fucking her all day yesterday.

Man! She looked so beautiful after all that sex. Her eyes twinkled. Her cheeks were pink and she just seemed to have a wonderful satisfied glow around her.

She was the best Christmas present he could ever have hoped for.

"I could spend the rest of my Christmases up here...with you," he admitted softly. "But only if you stop working for Kidnap Fantasies. I want you all to myself."

She smiled and he nearly came on the spot at the gorgeous burst of dimples exploding in her cheeks.

"With you, I won't need Kidnap Fantasies."

"I didn't say we'd give up Kidnap Fantasies...just that you stop working for them."

She got his meaning because her eyes widened and her mouth opened into an "O". The sight of her luscious lips parted like that made his cock throb for some more heavy-duty lip action from her.

Obviously, she saw his shaft hardening, because she shook her head slowly.

"We should go down and make Santana breakfast. And open the presents he brought for us yesterday, if only not to be rude."

"I'd rather be rude and stay in bed with you," Connor chuckled, and reached out to her.

He was ready to make love to her again but Tania's frown stopped him.

"What?" he asked.

"It's awfully quiet down there. I think I hear the car starting up."

"Can't be. He said he'd hang around today and take us to the airport tomorrow."

"Maybe we should check. Besides, I've worked up quite an appetite. I need food or I'll be totally helpless when you two decide to fuck me again."

"Helpless sounds good."

She giggled. "For you maybe."

They both jumped as the phone beside the bed rang. Connor reached for it.

"Hey, Connor! Merry Christmas!"

"Santana?" What the hell was he doing phoning?

"Just wanted to let you know what a great time I had."

"Where are you? I thought you were downstairs."

"On my way to my next assignment, man. Just wanted to let you know that while the two of you slept, I stocked your fridge, compliments of Kidnap Fantasies."

Connor blinked in confusion.

"I'll be by to pick you up in two weeks."

"Two weeks?"

Tania's head snapped up.

"Yep, so enjoy yourselves. Tell Tania we've cleared it with her boss so she doesn't have to worry about her job. Compliments of Kidnap Fantasies. Oh, and you'll find cross-country skis, a sled and tons more condoms for you to use or not to use under the tree. Don't want that

awesome mountain scenery to go to waste. Merry Christmas! Ho! Ho!
Ho!"

The line went dead.

Connor laughed. "I'll be damned."

"What?" she asked. Curiosity sparkled in her eyes.

"That was Santana on the phone."

"I thought he was downstairs?"

Connor shook his head. "Nope, you were right. He took off with
the car. Says we've got this place for another two weeks and for you
not to worry about your nursing job. Kidnap Fantasies has taken care
of everything. Consider it a Christmas present from them."

The smile on Tania's face was priceless and Connor found his heart
filling up with love and his balls becoming tighter.

"By the look in your eyes, I get the feeling I'm not going to be
getting any food for a while." Tania giggled.

"Nope, not for a long time, baby. Not for a hell of a long time."

The End

Want more Jan Springer Adult Romances?

Mini Catalog

Kidnap Fantasies Series

In the land of the rich and famous, the top-secret Kidnap Fantasies is the answer to discreet and naughty downtime.

Book One

Jade's Fantasy

When ex-downhill skier Jade's two sisters give her a Kidnap Fantasies questionnaire, Jade is aroused at the prospect of having no-strings fun in the sun with a stranger whose only job would be to fulfill her every intimate fantasy. Although she knows she's too shy to send it in, she secretly pours her deepest wishes into the questionnaire.

Soon the questionnaire mysteriously vanishes and Jade's fantasy man appears on her luxury yacht in the form of a sexy handy man who gives her an intimate toy-filled holiday she'll never forget.

_____

Book Two
Christmas Lovers
(can also be found in the Merry Ménage Kisses Boxed Set)
Sergeant Connor Jordan, wounded overseas and sent back to the States to recuperate, just cannot stop fantasizing about the sexy nurse who cared for him. When his brothers give him a holiday gift certificate to Kidnap Fantasies, a top-secret fantasy organization, Connor knows he'll use their gift, if only to help him forget his wickedly delicious attraction to Nurse Sparks.
Nurse Tania Sparks has always been purely professional with her injured soldiers...until sinfully sexy Connor Jordan enters her hospital. He makes her body throb with an intense desire she's never known

before. The last thing she wants is to get involved with the injured warrior. So what's a woman supposed to do to relieve her naughty frustrations? Call Kidnap Fantasies and have them supply her with a look-alike man who'll help her forget her sexy soldier...

When Tania and Connor unexpectedly come together at a secluded mountain chalet, their love explodes in a ménage of passion, sensuous desires and a happily forever after.

Contains ménage scenes.

Book Three

Zero to Sexy

Because Santana hides from something bad in his past he lives only for the moment and doesn't dare dream of a future. He exists within the sensual world of Kidnap Fantasies, a top-secret escort world where he explores his sexuality and enjoys pleasure with both men and women. But it is love at first sight the instant he sees Amy at his good friend's wedding. She's got future written all over her. He knows she is a hunger he must deny, so why is he whispering "you're mine" to her at the wedding?

The instant Amy Sparks sees the handsome African American at her sister's wedding, she knows in her heart that he's everything she's ever fantasized about in a lover, but before they can connect, he mysteriously disappears. Upon discovering he works for Kidnap Fantasies, she knows how he'll make all her intimate fantasies come true...

When Santana's next Kidnap Fantasies assignment turns out to be Amy, he knows he must protect her from his past and he can be with her only this one time...

Reader Advisory: Includes a sizzling ménage scene and some male on male sensual interaction.

Boxed Sets

SIX Erotic Romance Ménage Stories! INCLUDES A BONUS MÉNAGE EBOOK

BONUS Ménage BOOK "Cowboys for Christmas" book 1 of Jan's new Cowboys Online series. Jennifer Jane is getting THREE Cowboys for Christmas ~ What more could a girl want? Jennifer Jane Watson has spent the past ten Christmases in a maximum-security prison. The last thing she expects is to get early parole along with a job on a secluded Canadian cattle ranch serving Christmas holiday dinners to three of the sexiest cowboys she's ever met!

~

Step into The Key Club's Ménage Nights where naughty fantasies come true and two men are hotter than one. Includes FIVE bestselling The Key Club stories; Ménage, Marley's Ménage, A Merry Ménage Christmas, Sophie's Ménage and Jewel's Ménage.

The Key Club Series
Ménage - Book One

Sandwiched between constant deadlines, erotic romance author, Claire Miller, enjoys an occasional unwind at The Key Club...this time she's going to indulge in a yummy ménage.

Marley's Ménage - Book Two

Single soon-to-be mom Marley Madison has had some wicked cravings in her day, but being pregnant has made her cravings downright...naughty. She wants a sizzling ménage and she needs it bad.

A Merry Ménage Christmas - Book Three

Dr. Kelsie Madison can't remember the last time she's had no-strings sex and that's her clue she's been working way too hard. It's time to unwind at the Key Club by indulging in a yummy Christmas present for herself...a red-hot ménage.

Sophie's Ménage - Book Four

It's Spank-Me Ménage Night at the Key Club and Sophie is finally taking the plunge back into the spank scene...she didn't expect her two ex-boyfriends to be there too.

Jewel's Ménage - Book Five

She thought she would never trust a man again...
Until one rainy night two hunky truckers come to Jewel's rescue,
igniting delicious desires for a red-hot ménage a trios.

Jaxie's Ménage - Book Six

A close encounter with death pushes Jaxie into making one of her most intimate fantasies come true...

A Homecoming Ménage Christmas - Book Seven

Rachel has a very naughty secret and she's way too embarrassed to let anyone know about it. When The Key Club throws a Santa Fetish Ménage Night, it's almost too good to be true. She has to figure out how to participate without anyone finding out!

Pleasure Bound Box Set
The Complete Series
Books 1 - 6

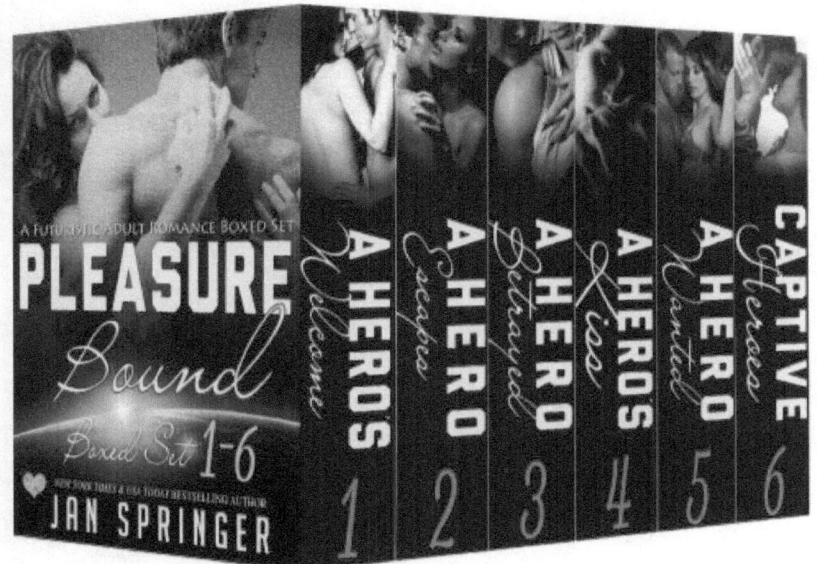

A Futuristic Adult Romance
Books 1-6

This PLEASURE BOUND BOXED SET is an EROTIC ROMANCE and includes the first SIX books in the Pleasure Bound series.

TOP-SECRET MISSION: Explore a recently discovered planet in outer space.

DISCOVERY: A sizzling trip into the realms of bondage, bdsm, pleasure-pain, betrayal and...love.

Inside this Boxed Set:
During a top-secret mission to a newly discovered planet, the six Hero siblings are thrust into a sensual world of erotic violence, unconventional romance and sizzling sex.

A HERO'S WELCOME

Pleasure Bound Book One

Jan Springer

Being shot and held captive isn't what astronaut Joe Hero had in mind when he agreed to a top-secret mission to explore a newly discovered planet for NASA.

But a man would have to be dead not to fall for the sensual female doctor in charge of his care.

One night of scorching passion in the arms of the stranger from another planet is enough to convince Dr. Annie there's more to males than she's been taught by the Educators.

Who is this sexy hunk and why does she welcome him into her bed and her heart *every* chance she gets?

A HERO ESCAPES

Pleasure Bound Book Two

Jan Springer

Queen Jacey has always fantasized about bedding a male.

But taking one for her enjoyment is strictly forbidden. That is, until an attractive well-hung stranger from another planet forces her to overcome her training and her beliefs.

Being held captive and forced to mate with a gorgeous Queen isn't exactly what astronaut Ben Hero expected when he agreed to explore a newly discovered planet for NASA.

Escaping *should* be his top priority but making sizzling love to Jacey *is* all he can think about.

When he discovers she's also being held captive, Ben's protective instincts kick in big time.

Suddenly they're on the run, irresistibly aroused, and wrapped in each other's arms every chance they get!

A HERO BETRAYED

Pleasure Bound Book Three
Jan Springer
Astronaut Buck Hero didn't count on being held captive or becoming
infected with passion poison when he agreed to explore a newly
discovered planet for NASA.
If he doesn't get the cure soon he's going to be one *very* dead man.
Fugitive on-the-run Virgin has just rescued an infected male and needs
to administer the cure - a twenty-four-hour sex marathon. Then she'll
turn him over to his enemies in order to gain her freedom.
But her well-laid plans go into orbit when she discovers she's fallen in
love with the stranger from another world.

A HERO'S KISS

Pleasure Bound Book Four

Jan Springer

During a secret NASA mission to locate their brothers on the faraway planet of Paradise, the Hero sisters become separated after they crash land...and find unexpected romance with the tormented male warriors of the species.

Jarod and Piper

Being injured and infected by sensuous swamp water isn't what Piper Hero signed up for when she agreed to search for her three missing brothers. But when she's rescued by a dangerously sexy man who makes her so hot that she can't even think straight, Piper is glad that she came.

Jarod Ellis has sworn off women. But he's captivated by Piper Hero, a woman who claims to be related to the Earthmen he has vowed to protect with his life. Although he mistrusts her, she sets free a carnal inferno of needs he's never experienced during his previous life as a pleasure slave.

Despite her intimate fantasies coming true, Piper knows she needs to continue her mission of reuniting her siblings and she'll do it-with or without the help of her well-hung stud...

A HERO WANTED

Pleasure Bound Book Five
(Loosely connected with this series)
Jan Springer

Old-fashioned gal needs a man who loves to walk in the rain. Must be well-hung. A homebody, white picket fence-type of guy. Sexual requirements-gentle yet untamed lover. He must be sexually adventurous who will train me to be same. Must be romantic, enjoy toys, interested in mutual light bondage, ménages are welcome.

That's what full-figured, antiques shop owner Jenna MacLean wants when she and her best friend outline a want ad just for fun on their weekly girls' night out.

After years of being away from his pretty-plus sized ex-girlfriend, Sully's back in town. When he finds the want ad, he knows he's the only man who can make all of Jenna's sizzling-hot fantasies come true. She's never left his heart and he needs her back in his bed-but he's not going the traditional romantic route. This time, he'll prove he loves her with help from the notorious Ménage Club, a relationship club designed specifically to get estranged couples back together with the help of a third and sometimes a fourth in the bedroom.

CAPTIVE HEROES

Pleasure Bound Book Six
Jan Springer

*During a secret NASA mission to locate their brothers on the faraway
planet of Paradise, the Hero sisters become separated after they crash
land...and find unexpected romance with the tormented alien male
warriors of the species in this ultra-long scifi book.*

Taylor and Kayla

While searching for her brothers, Kayla Hero is bound and imprisoned by the Breeders— along with a male captive whose tantalizing scars pique her interest. Forced to escape with him, she's irresistibly aroused when she suddenly becomes *his* captive. Wild lust flares in Kayla's eyes— a sensual side effect of the Fever Swamp water she's accidentally ingested. Taylor knows he will enjoy administering the cure — lots of sizzling hot lovemaking!

Blackie and Kinley

Injured and lost in a dense jungle, Kinley Hero is intimidated by the scarred man who hunts her, especially due to the power of erotic submission he holds over her.

Capturing his beautiful female prey, Blackie can't wait to train her as a pleasure slave for the Death Valley Boys. When her captor slips a collar around her neck, Kinley must struggle with lust as a natural submissive.

Shades of Ménage Boxed Set: Four Book Romance Ménage Collection

A fast-acting virus has killed a majority of the world's female population. Women's rights are stripped away and The Claiming Law is created, allowing groups of men to stake a claim on a female—as their sensual property.

After five years of fighting in the Terrorist Wars, the Outlaw brothers are coming home to declare ownership on the women they love...and they'll do it any way they can in **Jude Outlaw and The Claiming**.

PLUS

In the future...for population control, each human is embedded with a microchip that suppresses the urge to mate.

Centuries later,...A rebel group of young doctors are secretly tampering with their microchips and experimenting with intimacy. Now they search for allies who can help them with their cause – to eventually free humanity in the Dystopian Romance Ménage stories **"Perfect"** & **"Imperfect"**.

A CONTEMPORARY EROTIC ROMANCE BOXED SET
Naughty Girl Desires Boxed Set: Romance, Contemporary Romance, Romance Suspense, Box Set
(m/f only)

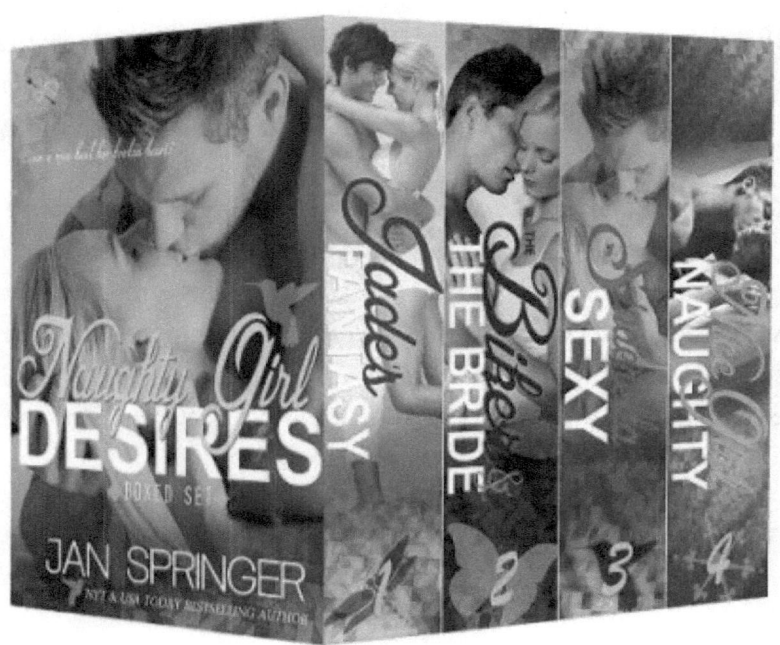

What You'll Find Inside Naughty Girl Desires
Jade's Fantasy
Kidnap Fantasies 1
Jan Springer
In the land of the rich and famous, Kidnap Fantasies is the answer to discreet naughty downtime.

When ex-downhill skier Jade Hart's two sisters give her a Kidnap Fantasies questionnaire, Jade is aroused at the prospect of having no-strings fun in the sun with a stranger whose only job would be to fulfill her every intimate fantasy. Although she knows she's too shy to send it in, she secretly pours her deepest wishes into the questionnaire. Soon the questionnaire mysteriously vanishes and Jade's fantasy man appears on her luxury yacht in the form of a sexy handy man who gives her an intimate toy-filled Christmas holiday she'll never forget.

~*~

The Biker and The Bride
Jan Springer

Wrapped in red-hot lust for revenge, Avery plots to murder the man responsible for the death of her son. Her plans are dashed when her ex-husband crashes her wedding and whisks her away on his motorcycle to the rustic Canadian wilderness cabin they'd once honeymooned.

Police detective, Mason is fighting for Avery's love with everything he has.

Armed with whipped cream, handcuffs and his undying devotion, Mason vows he will make Avery love again. But it's only a matter of time before the man she'd planned to kill hunts them down...

~*~

Sinderella Sexy
Jan Springer

By day, she's a dedicated gynecologist.
By night, Dr. Ella Cinder, escapes reality by secretly performing in her
own erotic, adult version of Cinderella, aptly re-titled Sinderella.
When sexy colleague Dr. Roarke Stephenson shows up in the
Sinderella audience on the same night her Prince Charming stands her
up, Ella seizes the opportunity to make Roarke into her Prince
Charming for one carnal night of extremely naughty fun in front of an
audience.
But at the strike of midnight, Ella knows she must face the harsh
reality that Roarke must never learn her secret life and they can never
be together again. Until then, she'll make sure he'll never forget their
night of sensual play.
Dr. Roarke Stephenson is immediately captured by the lusciously
curvy actress who hides behind a mask and is known only as
Sinderella. For some insane reason she reminds him of his klutzy
co-worker, Ella. But that's not possible. Ella would never have the
nerve to do the wickedly delicious things Sinderella does to him, or
would she?

~*~

Nice Girl Naughty
Jan Springer

Blind since nineteen, Summer has blossomed into a famous wood carver. When she's almost killed by a serial killer, she's whisked away to a secluded wilderness cabin by the man she once secretly loved. Summer can't get enough of touching professional bodyguard Nick Cassidy's thick, powerful muscles and all those other hard, yummy male body parts that she has always longed to explore.

For years Nick has stayed away from his best friend's kid sister, nice girl Summer. Now he's back, and sweeping his gorgeous redhead into the naughty cravings he's always had for her. With passion blinding him, Nick doesn't realize their hideout isn't safe—until it's too late.

Please note: The titles in Naughty Girl Desires have been previously published.

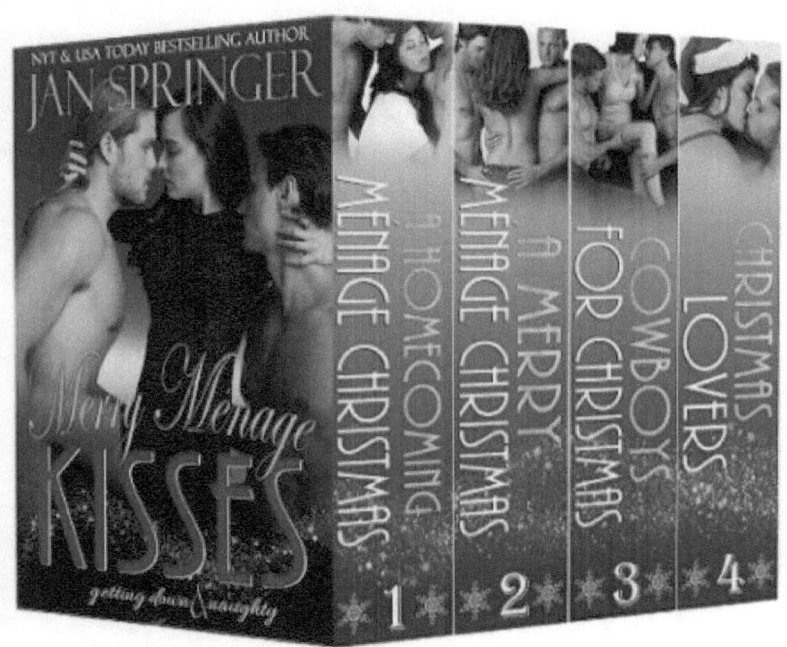

What You'll Find In The
Merry Ménage Kisses Boxed Set
Wrap yourself in four sexy holiday themed adult romance ménages.

A Homecoming Ménage Christmas

Jan Springer

Rachel has a *very* naughty secret and she's way too embarrassed to let anyone know about it. When The Key Club throws a Santa Fetish Ménage Night it's almost too good to be true. She *has* to figure out how to participate without anyone finding out!

Key Club bartenders Rob and Ron Simpson have fallen head over Santa hats for quiet, nice girl Rachel. But she has no clue how they feel about her. But she *will* know, because Rachel is coming home from a trip to Europe and the twin brothers are going to give her the best Homecoming Ménage Christmas ever. They'll do it with the help of some naughty toys, the Red Room, a safe word and...Santa Claus.

A Merry Ménage Christmas

Jan Springer

Dr. Kelsie Madison can't remember the last time she's had no-strings sex and that's her clue she's been working way too hard. It's time to unwind at the Key Club by indulging in a yummy Christmas present for herself. Something she's never experienced before - a red-hot ménage.

ER Dr. Ryder Greene and his roommate, physiotherapist, Dixon Flynn love sharing their women. They've had their eye on cute Dr. Kelsie Madison for quite some time, but she's a workaholic and she never has time to play.

When they learn she'll be at the Santa Claus Ménage Night festivities, they'll make sure they're the ones kissing Kelsie under the mistletoe. And if they get their wish, Kelsie will be taking them home for Christmas.

Cowboys for Christmas

Jan Springer

Jennifer Jane (JJ) Watson has spent the past ten Christmases in a maximum-security prison.

The last thing she expects is to get early parole, along with a job on a remote Canadian cattle ranch serving Christmas holiday dinners to three of the sexiest cowboys she's ever met!

Rafe, Brady and Dan thought they were getting a couple of male ex-cons to help out around their secluded ranch, but instead they get an attractive and very appealing female.

In the snowbound wilds of Northern Ontario, female companionship is rare.

It's a good thing the three men like to share...

They're dominating, sexy-as-sin and they fill JJ with the hottest ménage fantasies she's ever had. Suddenly she's craving cowboys for Christmas and wishing for something she knows she can never have...a happily ever after.

Christmas Lovers

Jan Springer

Sergeant Connor Jordan, wounded overseas and sent back to the States to recuperate, just cannot stop fantasizing about the sexy nurse who cared for him. When his brothers give him a holiday gift certificate to Kidnap Fantasies, a top-secret fantasy organization, Connor knows he'll use their gift, if only to help him forget his wickedly delicious attraction to Nurse Sparks.

Nurse Tania Sparks has always been purely professional with her injured soldiers...until sinfully sexy Connor Jordan enters her hospital. He makes her body throb with an intense desire she's never known before. The last thing she wants is to get involved with the injured warrior. So what's a woman supposed to do to relieve her naughty frustrations? Call Kidnap Fantasies and have them supply her with a look-alike man who'll help her forget her sexy soldier...

When Tania and Connor unexpectedly come together at a secluded mountain chalet, their love explodes in a ménage of passion, sensuous desires and a happily forever after.

Contains ménage scenes.

**For more Jan Springer stories, please visit
http://www.janspringer.com**

_____

Jan's Newsletter
Hi! If you would like to get an email when my books are released, you can sign up here:
Newsletter: http://ymlp.com/xguembmugmgb
Your emails will never be shared and you can unsubscribe whenever you like.

Discover Other Titles by Jan Springer http://www.janspringer.com

~*~

About the Author

Jan Springer writes full-time at her home nestled in cottage country, Ontario, Canada. She enjoys hiking, kayaking, gardening, reading and writing. She is a member of the Writers Union of Canada, Romance Writers of America. She loves hearing from her readers.

A Word From The Author

Hi! Thank you for purchasing this book. Word of mouth is important for any author to succeed. If you enjoyed this story feel free to leave a short review at the place where you bought it. I would really appreciate it. I look forward to bringing you more stories in the near future. Thanks!

If you would like to contact me or personally send me feedback, you can reach me by using my contact page at:

http://janspringerauthor.wordpress.com/contact/

Here are other ways we can connect:
Jan Springer Website at http://www.janspringer.com
Facebook - https://www.facebook.com/janspringereroticromance
Twitter - https://twitter.com/janspringer @janspringer
Pinterest - http://www.pinterest.com/janspringer1/
Jan's Blog - http://janspringerauthor.wordpress.com/blog-2/
LinkedIn - http://ca.linkedin.com/in/janspringerauthor/
Google Plus - https://plus.google.com/u/0/
101527334949931513035/posts
Jan's Newsletter - http://ymlp.com/xguembmugmgb
Goodreads - https://www.goodreads.com/author/show/
260628.Jan_Springer
Happy Reading,
jan springer

Don't miss out!

Visit the website below and you can sign up to receive emails whenever Jan Springer publishes a new book. There's no charge and no obligation.

https://books2read.com/r/B-A-WGQ-CTNG

BOOKS 2 READ

Connecting independent readers to independent writers.

Also by Jan Springer

Club Rendezvous
Shy Girl

Cowboys Online : Moose Ranch
Cowboys for Christmas
Cowboys In Her Pocket
Loving Her Cowboys
Cowboys in Her Heart
Always Her Cowboys

Intimate Secrets
Intimate Lover
Intimate Kisses

Kidnap Fantasies
Jade's Fantasy
Zero To Sexy
Christmas Lovers

Pleasure Bound
A Hero's Welcome
A Hero Escapes
A Hero Betrayed
A Hero's Kiss
A Hero Wanted
Captive Heroes

Pleasure Bound Boxed Set
Pleasure Bound : COMPLETE SERIES SciFi Erotic Romance Boxed Set

Tentacles Shifter Erotic Romance
Taken by Him

The Key Club
A Merry Menage Christmas
Sophie's Menage
Jewel's Menage
Jaxie's Menage

The Outlaw Lovers
Jude Outlaw
The Claiming

Colter's Revenge
Tyler's Woman
Resistance
The Outlaw Lovers
Alpha Outlaws Boxed Set

Vampira
Sweet Heat
Dark Heat
Wet Heat
Crimson Heat

Standalone
A Touch of Menage Boxed Set
Shades of Menage Boxed Set
Naughty Girl Desires Boxed Set
Nice Girl Naughty
Sinderella Sexy
The Biker and The Bride
The Fire Within
Bared to Him
Pleasure Bound : A Futuristic Adult Romance Boxed Set
Merry Menage Kisses Boxed Set
Inner Girl Rising
Stripped Naked
Risqué Girl Delights Boxed Set
A Holiday Menage
Ménage À Trois
A Hitman for Hannah
Billionaire Boyfriend

Edible Delights
Vampira
Toygasm

Watch for more at www.janspringer.com.